BEING HOSPITABLE

DESERT ROSE HOOKUPS

MEKA JAMES

CONTENTS

Acknowledgments   v

Chapter 1   1
Chapter 2   8
Chapter 3   14
Chapter 4   21
Chapter 5   27
Chapter 6   32
Chapter 7   38
Chapter 8   44
Chapter 9   51
Chapter 10   57
Epilogue   64

Thank you   69
About the Author   71
Other books by Meka   73

Cover Design by Avery Kingston

❀ Created with Vellum

ACKNOWLEDGMENTS

To Ginger, major thanks for being the "Official Lesbian" and giving me guidance with these characters. Your feedback and insight was invaluable.

To my RChat ladies...I wouldn't know what I'd do without you all. Your constant cheerleading and virtual shoulders to cry on help me more than you know. Special shout out to Lily Michaels and Evie Drae for your help in shaping Kiki and Charley's personalities.

To Mr. J whose goal in life is to make me happy. Thank you for being so supportive of my endeavours.

Lastly to the readers, without you I have no reason to keep sharing my words. Thank you for your support and hope you enjoy this story as much as I enjoyed writing it.

BEING HOSPITABLE

1

KIKI

A DEEP GROAN RUMBLED AT THE BACK OF MY THROAT AND I grabbed for the second pillow to cover my head.

The piercing dong of my doorbell rang out again.

"Fuck!" I tossed the pillow across the room and snapped my head to the side. Ten-thirty a.m., who the fuck was ringing my bell this early? I'd only been asleep for about an hour. The blackout shades kept my room dark so at least I didn't have to deal with bright sunshine off the bat. As I rolled from the bed, the screen on my phone lit up before my feet hit the plush carpet below. Charlotte's number flashed and those ten digits were a jolt of energy through my veins.

"Shit!"

I shimmied into a pair of shorts, somehow managing not to fall and bust my ass as I hurried from my room and down the stairs. The doorbell chimed again.

"I'm here. I'm here." I unlocked the door to be met with Charley's large grin and even larger big brother. Last time I'd seen her had been at her college graduation six months ago. And she looked just as good now has she had then. The sun hit her bright eyes, lighting up the umber hues, making them shine. Her normally relaxed hair had been done in long, faux locs that hung down mid-back. The form fitting pants she wore kissed the soft curve of her hips and the midriff—if it could be called that—shirt she wore barely had enough fabric to completely cover the small swell of her breasts. Every time she moved, the dark blue lace bralette she wore peeked from underneath.

Charley threw her arms around me. "Kiki, long time no see."

The action pulled my thoughts from going too far down the gutter. A place they had zero business even heading in relation to Charlotte Graham. Though not the first time they'd been there. The way she acted around me had started to change in the last year. Little comments here, small acts of what could be considered flirtation there. All of it baffling, but not something I'd let myself read into being more than an attempt to spread her wings.

Our weekend trip to Vegas in celebration of her graduation came to mind. Sharing a hotel room with her proved to be a test since she insisted on showering with the door open and walking around in the nude afterwards. A quick shake of my head dislodged the memory before it could fully form.

I stepped back and gave her a smile. "Yeah. Same."

My attention went to the large hunk of man behind her. Standing at least five-ten, and built like a linebacker though he'd never played a day in his life. People would look at him and never think he had a head for numbers or was an avid chess player. Two years into his job at Groundling Middle, he'd become head of the math department and spearheaded their award winning chess club.

Kenny and I became friends in middle school after we were paired together on a science class project. He'd thought he could coast through and have me do all the work. A fact he denied till this day. Work ethic aside, we'd bonded over sarcasm, practical jokes, and comic books.

"What up, Kiki?" he said, giving me a quick fist bump. He eyed me up and down. "You forgot didn't you?"

I scratched at my hair beneath its purple satin cap and stifled a yawn. "No. Not exactly." I stepped aside making room for them to enter. "Busy shift, plus I had to stay a little later at the station to finish some paperwork so I am wiped out. But the room is all ready."

Charley smiled at me. A warm, full stretch of her plump lips that put her deep dimples on display. "Thanks again for letting me crash here."

"Don't mention it."

When they'd called me last month asking if Charley could stay with me during her internship at Gosha Digital I'd agreed without a second thought. The timing worked out since I'd signed on the dotted line and bought my townhouse in Desert Rose Station four months prior. Kenny was my closest friend, and even though Charley was twenty-two, he still worried about her as if she was only sixteen. Opening up my second bedroom to her eased his mind, and saved her money.

Their dad died when Kenny was thirteen, and he'd stepped into the role becoming more father than older brother. I'd always felt bad for her because she could hardly date. Which was probably another reason she gravitated toward me more. If a guy even looked in her direction, Kenny was on him. Protecting her "future" was a big thing for him. He wasn't going to—in his words—let some dick fuck it up for her. As a result she hung out with us a lot. She'd managed to stay on the straight and narrow, graduated high school with honors, and received a partial scholarship to NAU.

She pulled me in for another hug. "I promise not to be too much hassle."

It could have been my imagination, but it seemed her hands

rested lower on my back and she held me longer than normal. Even in my half sleep state, I became acutely aware of her. The softness of her skin against mine, the mellow scent of shea butter and coconut oil. Her locs tickled the back of my hand. Even the quick rasps of her breath beside my ear. It all worked together to return my foggy brain down a path it had no business traipsing.

She was Kenny's baby sister. Not to mention straight. And completely off limits.

When she pulled away, she puckered her lips, and her eyebrows shot up quick almost like a waggle. "We're gonna have so much fun."

Yeah, I was tired. And confused. But crossed my arms in front of my braless chest to hide any possible reaction.

"Don't mention it. Um, you guys thirsty?"

I walked toward the kitchen while they got settled on my couch.

"Whose dog?" Charley asked.

I looked toward the slider. Sure enough, the beige little dog was walking back and forth sniffing around. "Oh, the lady next door. She never has him on a leash. I'm surprised he doesn't run off."

"He's cute," she commented.

"Eh, maybe you'll make friends with her then. Can't say that I've actually talked to any of my neighbors yet. The hours I keep aren't made for potlucks or block parties."

I pulled down three glasses from the cabinet and filled them with orange juice. As I handed them out, Charley brushed her fingers against mine when she took hers. The look she gave was hard to discern with my sleep addled brain, but whatever was happening set off warning bells.

"So, Kenny, how are you getting back?" I asked as I took a seat in my oversized chair far away from my new roomie.

"Derek is coming down and we're catching a Suns game

then riding back with him. Good thing it worked out for Princess here since she didn't have to make the drive alone."

Charley cut her eyes at her brother. "Don't put that on me, Kenneth. You damn near insisted on driving to make sure I arrived okay."

Kenny rolled his eyes but threw his hands up. It was a thing with them, anytime the full name came out, they knew the jabs were about to get serious.

"Fine, fine. But can you blame me? You've never done a long car trip on your own."

Charley crossed her arms. "And whose fault is that? You'll still be playing the over protective brother role when I'm forty and married off."

I laughed quietly to myself and sipped my juice. Being an only child meant I never had these sort of interactions. Sure, I played and sometimes fought with my cousins, but it wasn't the same thing as having a sibling. They were always going at each other, but she had a point. She was an adult and capable of taking care of herself, if given the chance. I suspected her staying with me would be the most freedom she'd had in a while. To save money she'd lived at home with Kenny and their mother instead of on campus.

"Depends on what kind of a knucklehead you end up with."

"Woah," I said butting in. "I'm surprised you didn't counter with her being in a convent or something."

"I know. See, I can be accommodating," he replied.

Charley chucked one of my red and white polka dot throw pillows at his head which he caught and tossed back at her.

"Kiki, so glad you offered to take me in. I feared he'd try and drive me back and forth, or worse find a short term apartment to share with me."

She ran her tongue along her bottom lip before a full smile stretched across her face. Her gaze lingered on me, giving me a return of the fuzzy thoughts from earlier.

"Mi casa es su casa."

Kenny's phone went off and he quickly checked the message. "Derek will be here in thirty." He fished keys from his pocket. "Let's get your stuff outta the car."

We followed him out to Charley's small blue hatchback. It was packed to the brim, suitcases, bags, loose items of clothing and shoes. You'd have thought she was moving in permanently instead of just three months.

After we'd lugged all her stuff up to what would be her room, Charley flopped backwards onto the bed, using Rufus as a pillow. The large, fluffy white stuffed dog was the only pet she'd been allowed to own due to her mom's allergies, aside from an unfortunate string of betta fish. Kenny had bought Rufus for her as sort of a joke, and she took to carrying it everywhere to get back at him.

"I can't believe you still have that thing?" I inclined my head toward the stuffed animal.

"Well, duh," she said sitting up and placing it in her lap. "He's my loyal companion. And completely house trained. He won't be any trouble at all."

"Yeah, I'm sure Ki will think he's the better of the two of you," Kenny chimed in, and was rewarded with her flipping him off.

"Anyway, this is nice, and I have my own bathroom." She stood and jutted her chin towards her brother. "No more sharing with that guy."

"Hey, I'm looking forward to not having all your girly shit and hair crap all over the place."

She shot him the bird again just as the doorbell rang. Our other buddy Derek stayed for about an hour before he and Kenny headed out for pre-game festivities. They could have that, sports was never my thing.

"If you want to get unpacked and settled have at it." I stifled a yawn. "I really need to catch a few hours of sleep, so sorry I won't be much of a host."

She linked her arm in mine and we climbed the stairs together. "No worries. And I promise to be quiet."

"No biggie. Once I fall asleep, I'm out like a light."

We got to the top of the second floor and she turned to face me. She twirled one of her locs around her finger and bit the corner of her lip before speaking. "I meant to ask, are you seeing anyone? I mean, I am sorta crashing in on you and all, so just wanted to know if I needed to make myself scarce sometimes."

I pressed my palms into my eyes then let my hands slide down my face. "Nice of you to be concerned about my privacy, but no, nothing to worry about on that front. With my schedule, maintaining a relationship is more effort than what I can put in right now."

Her face lit up at my answer. "Huh, well good."

I frowned.

She schooled her features. "I mean not good...not like that. More that I'm glad I'm not getting in the way..." Her words died out and she pulled her bottom lip in between her teeth.

I gave a little chuckle and shook my head. "No worries. All right I'm gonna hit the hay. Make yourself at home."

She leaned in and placed a quick kiss on my cheek. "Sleep well, and sweet dreams." With a finger wave, she turned and headed in the direction of the guest room.

Almost of their own accord, my eyes went down to check out the swing of her ass, round and plump beneath her capri yoga pants. *Holy hell, Kessla, you're checking out her ass.* Yeah, sleep. I needed sleep in the worst way.

2

CHARLEY

THE SCENT OF BACON AND COFFEE GREETED ME AS I HEADED down the stairs. Kiki sat at the peninsula sipping her drink and scrolling through her phone. She'd changed out of her uniform and now wore an Eeyore baseball T-shirt and matching shorts. Her beautiful, warm mahogany skin was a gorgeous contrast to the light pink clothing. Around her shoulders, her tight corkscrew, black coils hung free from the confining ponytail she'd wrangled them into before work.

"Mornin'," I said, stifling a yawn.

She jumped, set her cup down and swiveled to face me.

"Sorry, didn't mean to scare you."

She blinked once. Twice. And I saw the path her eyes took down my body before she spoke.

"Uh. No worries. Temporarily forgot I wasn't alone."

I kept her attention as I sashayed around the counter. I'd thought about slipping on pants or something, but instead opted to walk down in only my tank top and boy-short panties. These pair were great with the way they were cut shorter in the back so they showed off more of my ass. The fact that she checked me out told me I'd made the right call. I made a mental note, I wouldn't walk around full on nude like in Vegas, but wearing as little clothes as possible was certainly on the agenda.

"So, you're in the habit of making an entire pack of bacon for yourself?" I picked up one of the crispy strips and slowly closed my lips around it before I took a bite.

She shrugged and diverted her eyes. "I like bacon."

I opened and closed a few cabinets until I found the mugs and poured myself a cup of coffee. "I thought you'd be sleep."

She pressed her lips together and closed her eyes. A subtle, but definite shift in her demeanor. "Not a good night." She motioned in quick circles by her head. "Not ready to sleep yet."

I moved around the counter and ran my hand along her shoulders, giving a small tug so she leaned against me. "Wanna talk about it?"

She shook her head but wrapped her arms around my waist. I closed mine around her and held her. My fingers played in her curls and let her decompress from whatever she'd dealt with on her shift. My mind couldn't even process some of the things she'd probably had to deal with as an EMT. Being a first responder meant most times she saw people in their worst moments. It took a certain calling to handle jobs like that. I wasn't as squeamish as Kenny, but I also knew I was not capable of following our mother's footsteps into nursing, though she'd been hopeful. Being a hospital volunteer was a far cry different than putting in IVs or giving enemas.

We stayed there, with me giving her quiet comfort. My chest warmed from this small act of taking care of her. Being able to provide something she needed, even if it was as simple as a hug, I wanted to do it. Easing her stress, providing her with some sort of way to decompress, pleasing her any way I could, provided me with a sense of accomplishment. I massaged her head and she held me tight. After a few minutes she sat up and pressed her palms to her eyes.

"Sorry about that. Most times after a trying night I gorge on bacon and chill out until I can no longer keep my eyes open." Ki sucked in a long breath and let it out slow. She looked up and met my gaze. "But I'd forgotten the wonders a hug could do."

I squeezed her hand. "Hugs. Snuggles. Whatever you need, I got you covered."

When she gave me a sincere smile, my stomach did a flip.

"Thanks. I appreciate that."

I'd spent the last month counting down to this move. Not only did I get out from under my brother's overly watchful, and somewhat suffocating eye, I would get to spend three months with Kiki. Sure, I had my own friends, but anytime she'd come around, I'd always tried to be front and center, choosing to hang out with her and Kenny.

The little things she'd done over the years, I wasn't sure if she knew the huge impact they'd had. Being the voice of reason along with my mom when Kenny got to be particularly annoy-ing, the occasional hugs, and the genuine way she simply seemed happy to have me around—my lady boner for her grew with each instance. I had three months to have her see me as someone other than Kenny's sister.

I settled into the stool next to her. "Got any plans today? Other than sleeping at some point?" I turned just enough so that our knees touched.

"Uh, not really. I'm on a four on, three off schedule, so this is the start of my off. Typically I sleep and veg out on some TV. I don't have cable, but I do have a subscription service."

"That's cool."

She reached for another strip of bacon and I took a sip of my coffee and tried not to stare at her mouth for too long. So much time spent daydreaming about her lips. Wondering what they'd feel like on my skin. How she'd compare to others, better or worse than the drunk frat boys? Would she be as tentative as the couple of girls I'd fooled around with? Something told me no on that front.

Ki had always been confident and self-assured. She knew what she wanted and took very little shit from anyone, though she had a soft spot for me. At least it seemed that way with how she'd come to my defense. It could have been wishful thinking on my part, but I chose to believe otherwise. No, Ki would know exactly what to do, and what I needed at all times. I felt it in my bones. Just needed to get to the point where I could test my theory.

I shifted on my stool and tried to ignore the low tingle that started to build between my legs. Good thing I packed my toys. Living under the same roof with the woman who fueled many of my erotic dreams was going to have them being used in overdrive.

"You excited about your first day?" She slipped off the stool and carried her empty cup over to the sink.

The sleep shorts she wore clung to her ass so snug I wasn't sure she wore underwear beneath them. There were no discernable panty lines present. Just plump roundness on full display. When I glanced up she was watching me with brow arched and head tilted to the side. I probably should have been a little ashamed at getting caught, but I wasn't. However, the conversation I knew I had to have with her did make me anxious.

I rolled my tongue across my bottom lip and swallowed down the guilty lump in my throat. "Uh, yeah. Not sure if Kenny told you, but they only do three internship positions a year so competition was tough. If I bust my ass and outshine the other two, I could get a full-time job offer at the end of it."

Kiki's rich earthy eyes crinkled at the corners as her expression changed to joyful wonder. "What? That is fucking awesome. Well, a bigger congrats for getting in and I'm sure you'll blow the other two out of the water."

The sincerity and pride laced in her words set off a stream of warm fuzzies starting from my head and quivering down to my toes. If I was honest with myself, I'd worked my ass off during school and college so I could remain worthy of the praise and accolades she'd always given me. Sure Mom and Kenny were proud and would gush, but it had forever been different coming from Ki.

I bit the inside of my cheek and dropped my gaze down at my half full cup of coffee. The idea that she could possibly be disappointed nearly made me nauseous, but I couldn't avoid letting her in on the full story for too long.

"Yeah, well, it's a graduated internship. The first three months is the trial. After that we get an evaluation and one is cut but the other two are kept on for another six months."

My gaze fluttered back up at her and heat crept up my neck. The wait for a response stretched on and all the apologies I'd prepared for not being completely upfront ran through my head. In slow motion, Ki tilted her head to the side, rested a hip against the counter, and crossed her arms. After the awkward silence, she let out an airy laugh and stepped forward for another piece of bacon.

"That explains all the crap you brought along. The three months could actually be nine."

She didn't appear pissed off or disappointed in me. I pulled my lips inward and did a half shrug. With one eye closed, I squinted a sheepish glance in her direction. She chewed the bacon, slow and deliberate.

"Maybe," I squeaked out.

My heartrate spiked and the guilt of my fib to Kenny, which inadvertently became one to Kiki, set my ears a blaze, and concrete nerves weighted down my stomach. At the time, telling him it was only a three month stint seemed like a good idea. I mean, if I somehow made it past the first round, I could do some apartment hunting to find something so I wouldn't continue to impose on her. If she wanted me to, which I hoped wouldn't be the case.

"It's a paid internship, so I can help kick in with some rent. Buy groceries. Something. And I don't have to stay here the whole time."

She chuckled again and leaned forward, resting her forearms on the granite countertop. The loose collar of her shirt dipped down and try as I might to not, I stole a quick glance before I forced myself to keep eyes up on her lovely face.

"It's cool, I have the space so the room is yours for however long... but *you're* in charge of letting your brother know it'll be longer."

A nasally groan rumbled in the back of my throat. She straightened, held her hand up and shook her head to cut off my impending protest.

"I'm amenable to you staying as long as you need. I get it. But... if you want to have your independence or whatnot, you need to start by being honest. My only rule." She did air quotes around the last word.

I knew she was right. If I wanted Kenny to stop seeing me as a child, if I wanted Kiki to see me as more than his little sister, I needed to woman up and show them both I was very much an adult. I stood and stuck my hand out toward her.

"Deal. You're being hospitable, I can follow your one rule. I'm an adult. And I know what I want." I let my eyes roam down her body and quirked my mouth up on one side.

Her warm fingers wrapped around my mine and her rich eyes sparkled. "I'm sure you do."

3

KIKI

I FLOPPED TO THE SIDE AND PUNCHED MY PILLOW FROM BOTH sides. My efforts to get comfortable—and the even more futile attempt to not have severely inappropriate thoughts of Charley run through my head—kept me awake. We'd spent the day together hanging out and ninety-eight percent of that time she'd worn nothing more than the thin tank top and bright fuchsia underwear.

The fact she kept flirting—or seemed to be flirting with subtle brushes of her fingers against my leg and sitting closer than necessary—added to my state of restlessness. Then there was the moment, the soft swipe of her fingers when she'd swiped them along the side of my mouth to remove a crumb. An overwhelming urge to kiss her attacked me, and it took amazing mental gymnastics to snap my senses back under control.

What the hell was wrong with me?

Charley and I had always had a connection, but I never thought much of it. She was sweet and funny. Honestly, she had one of the most bubbly and infectious personalities of anyone I associated with. Me being on the more reserved side of life, it was one of the qualities I admired about her. But now it seemed that free, and open outlook on life was aimed directly at me and leading down a path that could have major repercussions.

I flopped again, lying on my back and stared up at the ceiling. I flung the covers off and stretched out spread eagle. Relief, that's what I needed. To work off some of this damn tension. I let my eyes drift closed and slid my hands along the sides of my breasts. I pushed them together, and grazed my palms over my protruding nipples.

I rubbed in small circles, letting myself get lost in the sensations. My breathing mellowed and I focused on the slow building. My thoughts wandered to shapely legs and a round ass covered by fuchsia panties that rode high in the back.

Eyes wide, and heart pounding, I shot straight up in bed. Charley. I was fantasizing about Charley. Kenny's younger sister. Sweet, off-limits, and straight Charley.

I needed to get myself together. With a groan I rolled from the bed and padded across my room needing a nice cold drink. Maybe a strong one.

When I opened the door, I stopped at the sound of a low buzz coming from across the hall. Charley's door was cracked and a sliver of light cast across the floor. The sound—constant and familiar—came accompanied by a soft moan. Well fuck me, she was... no I didn't need that mental picture forming in my head. Closing the door is what I should have done, not open it wider so I could hear better.

The buzz got louder, then faded away. Clear as day I could picture her movements of pushing whatever toy in then pulling it back out as she pleasured herself. I shook my head to dislodge the thoughts, though my body had other ideas. Her tantalizing moans increased as did the ticking, slow pulse between my legs. The rise and fall of my chest scraped my hardened nipples against my soft, cotton T-shirt.

Why could I perfectly envision her lips slightly parted? Eyes closed. Nude body with legs spread wide. I squeezed my own eyes shut and pinched the bridge of my nose. My other hand gripped the doorknob, and I tried to ignore the dampness of my panties. Tingling aches danced through my fingers as I fought the urge to relieve the mounting desire. I contracted and released the muscles of my pussy, the action adding to my growing horniness. Her moans came faster.

This was wrong. I went to push the door closed when a single, breathy word stopped me.

"Kiki."

***

I'd been awake for nearly an hour, yet I couldn't make myself get up. It'd been twenty minutes since I'd heard Charley's phone ring, followed by a muffled conversation. After that the low creak of her door opening signaled she was fully up and downstairs. All while I basically hid in my room trying to figure out how to face her after eavesdropping last night.

And the fact she'd masturbated while thinking about me.

There needed to be a conversation. But what?

"Fuck it," I grumbled and tossed the covers aside.

This would only be weird if I made it weird. I could pretend last night hadn't transpired. I could. Besides, it's not like she knew I'd heard her. She was more than entitled to her privacy and her fantasies, even if they apparently included me. And even if I'd finally fallen asleep last night dreaming of her. Charley was off limits. I had self-control, though lord knows she seemed to be testing it at every turn.

I was an EMT. A job made for people who were able to keep cool heads no matter the situation. I handled things from fucking gunshots, to stab wounds, and falls from five stories, I could more than handle the little minx that now lived with me.

After slipping on a pair of capri-length yoga pants, I took a deep breath and headed downstairs.

Charley's ass greeted me. Bent over as she reached into the oven, and covered barely by orange panties with "Spank Me" written across the back in white letters. A slow exhale passed through my lips and I swallowed the dry lump in my throat. What I wouldn't give to accommodate the novelty request.

What the hell?

Sleep deprived. I was still massively sleep deprived. That had to be my only excuse. Fantasizing about her was bad enough. But adding her being over my knee, bare-assed, and my hand warmed from swift blows to her backside was a whole new level of fucked up wrongness.

A quick shake of my head, and I cleared my throat.

She turned and smiled, putting her deep dimples on full display, when she saw me. "Perfect timing." The pan in her hand contained steaming cinnamon rolls.

The sweet scent of which finally made its way through my consciousness, along with the deliciousness of hickory smoked bacon and dark roast coffee. She'd made breakfast. She'd prepared a meal, for me. Well us, but, still, she'd gone through the trouble. She'd always thought of others with a need to take care of everyone else. Maybe it was because she, Kenny, and her mom became a much tighter unit after Mr. Graham's passing. Regardless of the reason, Charley had a giving personality and her making breakfast was a gesture that I appreciated.

I slid onto one of the stools as she started icing the rolls. "Thanks for cooking. You didn't have to do that."

The corner of her mouth lifted to the side. "I wanted to. One of the ways I can please you." She winked, then rushed to add, "Since you're letting me stay here and all."

I studied her for a moment, her locs were pulled back, covered by a multicolored scarf, knotted at the top. The black, midriff tank she wore barely covered her small breasts and if she moved the wrong way, there would be a wardrobe malfunction. One I wouldn't...no, no, and no. I would not let that train of thought take hold. And I would not read anymore into her "please me" comment.

I reached for a piece of bacon and tore my gaze away from her shirt. The bite I'd just taken lodged in my throat and caused a choking cough that had Charley around the counter and patting me on the back.

"You okay?" She left to fill a glass with water and set it in front of me.

I tried not to look at her. The back of her panties had nothing on the "Kiss Me" wording located on the front, perfectly placed at the sweet V of her legs. I took a gulp and gave my chest a few pats.

"You good?" she inquired again.

I nodded and cleared my throat a few times. "It went down the wrong way."

She cast another concerned look at me then sashayed back around the counter to finish putting the icing on the cinnamon rolls. "Want coffee?"

"Yeah... but I'll get it," I added quickly. With that shirt and her having to raise her arms to reach into the cabinet. No. I needed to not have any more inappropriate images of her in my head. I was likely going to hell for the ones I already harbored. I was going to need to spend some extended time with my showerhead later.

"Aw'right." She bit the corner of her lip and started humming to herself and bouncing along to the low tune.

I stood and diverted my attention before I let myself get sucked away in the mesmerizing jiggle of her boobs. "I have to grocery shop today, so make a list of anything you need." I kept my eyes focused on pulling down the mug and on pouring the steaming, dark liquid into it.

From the corner of my eye, I saw her turn and rest back

against the counter. I mimicked her action. Even with the generous amount of space between us, my kitchen seemed to shrink in size. Why the hell was I so affected by her? Even with her acting like a nudist in Vegas, I'd managed to keep sexual thoughts at bay. Mostly. But now, from the moment she'd stepped into the house, she was on my mind.

"Can I go with you instead?" Charley brought the butter knife to her mouth and licked.

I tightened my hand around the handle of my cup and worked to keep breathing at a normal rate. The "Kiss Me" on her panties called to me and I found myself wanting to give in to both sayings.

"Uh... that's cool." The words managed to find their way around the dry lump in my throat.

The way her tongue moved to clean the other side of the knife had me wanting to take the utensil's place.

I put down the untouched cup of joe. "I'm gonna go take a quick shower."

She stepped into my path. "Ki, I have another confession." With a lick of her lips, she closed in, shortening the space between us, and sucking the air from my lungs in the process.

"You moving in on a more permanent basis?" I tried to keep my voice light and joke about her surprise news from yesterday. All while ignoring the fact she stared me down like I happened to be on the menu for the morning, and not minding at all if that was actually the case.

Her deep dimples made an appearance as a bright grin broke free. That look was adorable and trouble all wrapped up in one. The desire to take care of her and provide her with countless reasons to smile at me like that danced through my head. My heart could easily have been in competition at the Indy 500 with the rapidness at which it raced. Why the hell did she make me so nervous? *Because she's off limits Kessla. Off limits. Off limits. Off limits.* I repeated the mantra to myself while she steadily inched closer until we stood damn near nose to nose. Sexy, beautiful, vibrant. Charley was all that and more. She may have been off limits, but damn if I didn't want her. She was temptation.

"This might be over stepping, but... I want to kiss you."

4

CHARLEY

HER SUDDEN INHALE WAS AUDIBLE. KIKI STARED AT ME, MOUTH slightly agape, and her beautiful warm brown eyes dilated to epic proportions. A flurry of bumble bees attacked my stomach, stinging and prickling at my senses. I'd told myself to wait, flirt more, but fuck it, like she'd said yesterday, if I wanted something, I needed to speak up. And I wanted her, but more I wanted her to want me.

She did a slow tilt and the center of her brow creased. "I'm sorry, what?"

Too late to back pedal now. I swallowed, hoping to gather moisture in my desert dry mouth all while praying the obnoxious loud beating of my heart was all in my head and not something she could hear.

I let my tongue make a slow path along my bottom lip, and lifted my chin slightly and spoke each word with deliberate intent. "I. Want. To. Kiss. You."

Kiki's chest rose, then fell with the slow inhale and drawn out exhale. "That's... not a good idea."

Not exactly the reaction I'd expected. "Why not?"

She narrowed her eyes and pressed her lips into a tight line.

Lips that should be on mine. I couldn't have been that off in my feelings. The way she looked at me. How she checked me out when she didn't think I saw. She had to be as into me as I was into her. I couldn't have been that off.

She schooled her features and stepped back. "Aside from the obvious reason?"

My turn to be confused. "I can't think of any obvious reason." I let the one possibility I wanted to ignore sink into my awareness. "Unless you aren't as into me."

Mentally, I crossed my fingers and said a silent prayer that wouldn't be the reason.

A ghost smile lifted the corners of her mouth. "That is not it. Quite the opposite in fact."

The vindication that hit me after her words was short lived because of the ones that followed.

"Your brother. For starters."

The best way to throw an ice bucket on my raging libido. Shit. *And for starters? For starters?* Hell, Kenny was enough of an obstacle, well her loyalty to him. And it's not like I wanted to cause an issue, but damn I wanted her. Had for years and I was done letting my brother be a road block. What more could there be?

I closed the space she'd created. A bold move, but I couldn't give up yet. We stood so close I could feel the whispered caress of each tiny exhale she made. "We." I gestured between us. "Are two consenting adults." I stressed the last word. "Who I sleep with is no concern to Kenneth."

She laughed. Yeah, I knew after years of being around us she'd see through that bullshit line. It didn't make it any less true. I loved my brother, and I appreciated his support and protection over the years, but I needed to come into my own. I needed the freedom to date and maybe screw up along the way. I wanted to grow and explore life, love, and a deeper intimacy.

And I wanted to do those things with the woman standing in front of me.

"Do you find me attractive?"

"Very." She answered without hesitation.

"Okay. Same. So, if I wasn't your friend's younger sister would you fuck me?"

Again she answered without delay. "Yes."

Her eyes traveled the length of my body before meeting mine again. I pulled my shoulders back which pushed my chest forward. Small, but mighty, boobs were a secret weapon. Well, not so secret when the person of your desire had them too. But with the drop in her gaze, the action was still just as effective.

She reached out and placed a hand on my hip. The pads, a touch calloused, but still soft, skated along my hip bone and traveled the length of the waistband of my panties. My eyes fluttered closed at the much anticipated intimate touch.

Then it was gone.

"But you are his sister."

Damn it! He was a major cock block and he wasn't even here. That was some shit. But not a total loss. Kiki was into me. She wanted me as much as I wanted her. A smile pulled at my lips and I ran my fingers along the same path hers had taken. The fact that she hadn't walked off and the fact that her eyes watched my movements told me this wasn't over.

"Ki, I want you. I have wanted you for a while."

She frowned again and shook her head. "What are you talking about?"

My nipples were so hard they ached. My pulse raced with a mixture of lustful anticipation and what-the-hell-was-I-doing nervousness. And my pussy... it tingled with a longing that only she could sate.

"I'm talking about the fact that my attraction to you isn't a brand new thing. I mean did you think I walked around nude in Vegas for my health?"

She rolled her eyes and shook her head. "Well, mine towards you is. Or at least acknowledging it. I noticed. Man, did I ever notice that something had changed...but thinking of you as anyone other than Kenny's sister isn't something I've allowed myself to do."

I rolled my tongue along the roof of my mouth as I processed her statement. I'd be lying if I said it hadn't stung, but I guess I understood. Still, the underlying rejection burned in the back of my throat. I had zero control over my family connections.

I stepped back. "So, because of who I'm related to, you'd deny yourself something you want? Even knowing I want the same thing?" A slight hitch cracked my voice as I asked the question. The frustration threatened to strangle all the remaining hope and leave it shriveled up like a dusty tumbleweed.

She rested against the counter. "About that. You and I have talked before about this *boy* or that *boy*..."

She let the comment hang in the air, but put emphasis on each "boy." I bit the inside of my cheek to suppress the smile threatening to break loose. With my hands out to the side I did a nonchalant shrug. "I like them too. Was that your other hang-up?"

Her only response was a subtle nod.

I licked my lips and drew air into my lungs. "Does it ease your mind if I tell you, you won't be my first?"

A smirk pulled at her full lips. "A little."

There was a twinge of possibility hanging between us. Yes, she had reservations, mostly because I was Kenny's sister, but she hadn't walked away. She hadn't quashed the discussion, and hadn't turned me down outright.

What she had done was openly take in all I'd purposefully put on display. Each time her eyes lingered on the front of my panties, I got added encouragement to keep pleading my case. To me, Kiki and I were a very logical choice.

Kenny's concerns were on me being hurt, or used. Someone taking advantage. There was zero worry of that happening with Ki. I couldn't be in better hands. Literally and figuratively. And boy did I want to be in her hands. And at her beck and call. My body burned hot and my mouth ran dry. We stared at each other. The lusty need palpable, so thick it seeped into my every pore.

I shifted my weight, widening my stance, and crossed my arms under my breasts. It was time to put it all out there and go for broke. "Last night I couldn't sleep. I tried, but I was a pent up ball of horniness."

She took in a shuddered breath, her lips parted, and she reached behind her to grip the countertop.

Her reactions gave me the bravado to keep going. "Do you know what I did?"

She blinked slowly and the side of her mouth hooked upward. "I might have some idea, but I want you to tell me."

The husky tenor in her words was a direct jolt to my pussy. Did she hear me? The thought of that made me feel naughty in the best possible way. I wanted to touch her, to bury my face in the crook of her neck, and run my palms over her firm breasts. To lick, nip, and suck any and all parts of her glorious body. Make her happy, to please her. Like last night, the possibilities had me dripping.

I kept my eyes on Ki when I started making circles around my hard nipples. She wanted to hear and doing what she wanted drove me to recount my night in the most seductive way. "I couldn't stop thinking about you, so I stripped down and spread out on the bed."

I moved my hands under my shirt and squeezed. She stood straighter and gripped the counter harder.

"I imagined your hands on my body. Much like I'm doing

now. I wanted you to pinch my nipples to the brink between pain and pleasure. Until I was squirming for a relief I didn't really want."

Kiki ran her tongue along the front of her teeth, and with a smile that shot lightening through my body, she stepped forward and erased the space I'd created.

"Then what?" She stroked my waist. The gentle touches left a line of goosebumps in their wake. My insides clenched.

I licked my lips and slid one hand down my stomach. My pulse raced. Everything I'd dreamed of was within reach. Here, with her, relaying my desires, my body was alive with adrenaline and lust surging through me.

"I thought about how you'd kiss your way down my body. The idea made me so wet. I touched myself. My pussy was so needy, eager for attention, but it wasn't enough. It wasn't what I wanted." My fingers grazed just below the waistband of my panties. I leaned forward and whispered against her ear. "Wasn't who I wanted. Who I want."

Close. So close her protruding nipples brushed against mine.

I drank in her appearance. Smooth, dark skin. Stunning rich eyes. Full, plump lips.

Her warm fingers wrapped around my wrist and pulled my hand free. Slowly, she shook her head and bent my arm behind my back. An action that brought our bodies closer. She worked her thigh between my legs, and I groaned when she rubbed it against my needy sex. The friction divine, but not nearly enough.

"Where exactly would you like that kiss?"

5

KIKI

THE LOGICAL PART OF MY BRAIN SCREAMED NO. THIS WAS NOT A good idea. But louder was my attraction to the sexy woman in my arms.

Charley used her free hand to tap against her lips. "Here. For now."

Beautiful. Coy. The apple in the Garden of Eden. My lips met hers and the taste was the sweetest of all forbidden fruits. I groaned against her and drove my tongue forward in a desperate need to have more of all she offered.

Our joined hands tightened, and her other free one tangled in my hair pulling me close, and giving as good as she got. Mine grabbed a handful of her firm ass. Pebbled nipples rubbed against me and I pressed my thigh harder between her legs. Her damp panties, clear evidence of all she'd said, drove my own arousal to new heights.

My heart hammered in my chest. The pulsating between my legs beat in a needy rhythm for more. I kissed her harder, letting myself drown in the perfection of the moment. A tiny voice in the back of my mind told me to pull away, to stop before things got more out of hand.

Charley was the one to put on the brakes. She pulled back, her heaving chest matched my own. Without a single word, she pulled the scrap of fabric masquerading as a shirt over her head. All air left my lungs at the beauty before me. Breasts pert, nipples puckered and begging to be sucked.

"You. Are. Dangerous," I said with an airy chuckle.

She hooked her thumbs in the waist of her underwear. "Who? Lil' ole' me?"

The slow shake of my head matched the slow nod of hers. She stood before me naked and wearing only a confidence that fit her well. My gaze settled on the apex of her legs. Smooth, bare, glistening, and beckoning me for a taste. A small voice of reason sounded off, warning me to not go down the road of temptation.

A five alarm fire burned through me. My pussy clenched with wanton need to feel her skin to skin.

I stepped forward and placed my hands on her waist and caressed the soft flesh. "Is this what you want?"

Charley licked her lips then snaked her hand between our bodies. My mouth went dry when she stroked herself. Two fingers disappeared inside her folds, and then she pulled them free and held the wet digits in front of me.

"What do you think?"

I wrapped my hand around her wrist and slid her coated digits into my mouth. The first tastes of her hit my buds. A decadent, tangy delight. A mere sample that made me want it straight from the source. I glided her fingers in and out, slipping my tongue between them until I was satisfied they were clean. But I needed more.

With that thought in mind, I walked her backwards, out of the kitchen and over to the living room. Her fingers danced across my abdomen. Mine rested on her hips. Our gazes locked. Tiny circles and tentative movements as she inched upwards until she reached her intended target. As her hands went higher, so did my shirt and my heart rate. With my top removed, a giant smile graced her beautiful face.

The heavy weight of arousal anchored between my legs. I let my fingers trail up and down her sides. We stood damn near eye to eye. Charley wasted no time in palming my now exposed breasts. Using her thumbs, she made tiny circles around my taut nipples. I let my hands slip around the small of her back until they cupped her ass. My neglected libido went into overdrive when she dipped her head and drew one of my aching nipples into her mouth.

Fiery, wet heat made my pussy clench as she squeezed while flicking her tongue against the tight bud. The blood pounding through my veins thumped a rhythmic beat between my legs. Charley switched sides. Her warm mouth lavished attention on one nipple while she pinched and tweaked the other.

I slid one hand around, searching for then finding the slickened prize between her legs. The heavenly velvet softness of her body surrounding me was almost too much to handle. Cool air hit my sensitive nipples when her mouth abandoned it, but her thumbs continued to make circles around the erect peaks.

Moving my free hand up to the nape of her neck, I pulled her closer for another feverish kiss. Her low moans vibrated against my lips. In her silky warmth, my fingers glided back and forth with ease. The heady scent of arousal mingled in the air. I suckled her tongue and groaned when her heated palms squeezed my breasts and pinched my nipples with practiced expertise.

As her desire ran down my fingers and my own pooled in my panties, time for the slow tease had passed. I pulled away and with a gentle shove, she fell backwards onto the couch. I dropped to my knees in front of her and pushed her legs wider. My heart rate spiked at the sight of her open, ready, and waiting. I dove in, curling my tongue upwards, licking her from bottom to top. The taste of her made my eyes flutter and my entire being hum with delight.

In rapid fire, I flicked my tongue over her stiff bud. A strangled purr was my reward. And it was a fucking sexy as hell sound. One I needed to hear again. I made small circles between the parted soft folds and slowly slid in two fingers. Charley lifted her hips, pushing her sweet pussy upwards against my tongue.

I pulled back to look at her. Mouth parted, eyes half closed. She palmed and squeezed her breasts. Tweaking her own nipples and moaning at the sensations created. I continued to stroke her as her walls constricted around my hand in waves. When I licked my lips, the essence of Charley again hit my senses.

My actions sped up as I moved my fingers in and out of her body. Bringing the stunning woman splayed out before me to climax became my driving need. I descended on her again, closing my lips around her stiff clit, sucking the tiny bud.

"Holy fuck." Charley shifted and propped her feet up on the couch.

The move opened her to me increasing my access to all things gloriously Charley. Blood pounded hot in my ears, leaving me lightheaded and dizzy, drunk on pleasure. My own panties were soaked, and the throbbing need between my legs pumped with the rapid beat of my heart.

Her breathing turned to pants and low whimpers poured from her lips. I needed to see, to watch her come undone. To watch and know I was the reason for it. Charley arched her back, and I kept pace moving my digits within her body. I used my other hand to add pressure to her swollen clit, rubbing in fast circles. She rotated her hips in rhythm to my actions. Faster she went until she stopped. Her legs shook and she let out a long drawn out groan. A tidal wave of vibrations accompanying her orgasm clenched around my fingers.

My chest heaved, the action scraped my aching nipples against the cushion and served to drive my need higher. I gave a slight pinch to her clit, which made Charley thrash and pump her hips upwards.

"Ki! Oh... oh god..."

I kept finger fucking her. The steady rocking in sync with my movements offered encouragement. She wanted more just as much as I wanted to give it to her. The second hit. Her legs gave out and drooped off the edge of the couch. She shook her head from side to side as her body jerked with short convulsions. With a parting kiss, and final swiped to her sex, I removed my fingers, and moved up to sit beside her.

She collapsed into my lap and draped a weak arm across her face, covering her eyes. I traced the outline of her areola and she shuddered from the touch.

"Fucking hell, Ki."

6

CHARLEY

I HUGGED KI'S PILLOW, BRINGING THE DOWN SOFTNESS CLOSER TO my face, inhaling her faint scent. Now that my internship had kicked off, Ki and I had barely seen each other during the week. We may have managed an hour, hour and a half, tops combined over the last five days.

Memories of our amazing day together fueled me through the absence. The feel of her hands on my body popped to the forefront of my mind. I bunched the covers between my legs. Arousal crept through as I remembered once more her expert use of her tongue as she licked, sucked, and finger fucked me into oblivion. I rocked against the comforter and let out a low groan.

Even more enticing was the memory of turning the tables. Being allowed to explore her body in return...real life had nothing on the fantasies. Hearing her breath catch and witnessing her falling apart because of something I was able to do for her. I squeezed my legs to create more friction.

"Charley?"

I sat up and met Kiki's surprised gaze. I tucked the blanket around me. Embarrassment bloomed at the idea of her catching me mid dry-hump of her bedding. "Mornin'."

She stepped close to the foot of the bed, cocked her head to the side, and crossed her arms. "What are you doing in here?"

I diverted my gaze down to the paisley patterned comforter. *Shit, I'd overstepped.* "We...um, we haven't seen much of each other."

I crawled toward her. Seeing her, and knowing we had two full days together, my heart sped up. I rose up on my knees and placed my hands on her waist.

Head down, I stole a peek at her through my lashes. "I wanted to be here to welcome you home."

A slow smile stretched across her face. "You did?" She cupped my cheek and gently made me look at her.

That smile, the sound of surprised happiness in her voice eased the knot which tried to form.

I nodded and moved my hands up to slowly start undoing the buttons of her blue work shirt. She didn't stop me.

"I missed you."

Her gaze dropped to my hands.

A second button was released. "We can have a nice shower."

The image of her body wet and glistening under a spray of water flipped through my head clear and bright.

"We?"

I glanced up from my task to stare into her deep, warm brown eyes. "Yes. I'm sure you've had a long night. I want to help wash away your stress, then we can snuggle until you fall asleep."

Her hands wrapped around mine, stilling my actions.

"What are we doing, Charley?"

I inched closer, working hard to keep my smile at bay. "Well, um, after last Sunday, I was sure you already knew about the birds and the bees."

Ki rolled her eyes and flashed her pearly whites. She used her thumbs to caress the inside of my wrists. "You know what I mean."

With a huff, I sat back on my heels and crossed my arms over my breasts. Breasts that longed for the hot wet heat of her mouth. A mouth I apparently wasn't going to be experiencing this morning.

"This again? I was pretty sure that hang-up was in the rearview."

Ki pinched the bridge of her nose and rolled her shoulders. Meanwhile, I saw all my hopeful plans for the next two days floating away.

"I know. I know." She looked at me straight on. "Sunday was nice... No, scratch that, more than nice. Nice is an insult to what happened. But..."

I held up my hand and cut her off. Last thing I wanted to hear tumble from her luscious lips was any possible mention of regret.

I scrambled off the bed. "Save it, Ki. It's all good."

I wasn't in the habit of throwing myself at someone that didn't want me. Before I could let the sting of rejection swell to allergic proportions, she wrapped her arms around my waist and pressed me against her soft body.

"I'm sorry. I wasn't trying to piss you off." Ki's tone was soothing, as if she were trying to placate my tantrum.

Her hold was snug, but not restrictive. Not that I wanted free, despite my hurt feelings. Being held by her felt safe. Secure. Exactly everything I needed.

"I didn't take you for the wham, bam, thank you ma'am type."

Warm air blew across my cheek from her quiet laugh. She placed a kiss on the side of my neck and tightened her arms.

"I'm not. That's the problem."

I swiveled and snaked my arms around her neck. I chewed the inside of my cheek and let myself get lost in the smoldering kindness of her eyes.

"So, I'm not a one off?"

She rolled her tongue along her bottom lip and her hands moved lower until they firmly cupped my ass.

"If I remember correctly, you got off more than once."

The grin that broke out on my face could have split it in two. I pressed my body tighter against her. "Same could be said about you."

My hardened nipples scraped against the fabric that separated us. Giving a small tug, I pulled her face closer until our mouths met. I wasted no time in pushing my tongue forward. It collided with hers and they jockeyed for control that I happily relinquished to her.

God, kissing this woman was a dizzying experience. One I already found myself addicted to. Her fingers dug into my ass, kneading and squeezing handfuls of my flesh. The action brought me even closer and I attempted to grind against the baggy cargo-pants she wore. She pulled back allowing both our lungs to replenish the stolen oxygen. My body mourned her absence when she released her hold and stepped away.

"I need to shower. Go get it warmed up and I'll be in to join you." The command was accompanied with a tight squeeze to my butt followed by three "move-it-along" pats.

A command. There was no question there. It wasn't a request. It was an order, one I happily obeyed. I all but skipped off toward her attached bath, gathering my exposed locs as I began twisting them into a makeshift bun.

She cleared her throat. "Um, do all your panties come with little messages?"

I stopped and twisted so I could read what was across my ass. "Bad Girl." A slow smile pulled at my lips as I turned to face her. "Maybe." I stuck my thumbs in the elastic waistband and slid them back and forth. "If you're lucky, you'll get to find out."

One corner of her mouth lifted to the side and she took slow steps to close the distance between us. "'Bad girls' get spankings. And if I remember correctly, you have a hot little pair that asks for just that."

Her words cranked up the simmering arousal between my legs to a full inferno. I'd dabbled in a little role play here and there. Naughty Schoolgirl, Doctor and Nurse. All just for fun, but never allowing my full desires out in the open. But with Ki, holy fuck, her words may have been playful, but unless it was all in my imagination, there could be more. And that thought sent a zing of thrill ping-ponging through my body.

With a step forward, I erased the remaining gap between us. I kissed her chin and went back to the task of unbuttoning her shirt.

"Damn it! You wear entirely too many layers," I complained once I got her shirt open only to be faced with a form fitting tank and what was sure to be an unflattering sports bra beneath that.

She shrugged. "Hazard of the job. Layers are needed. I've had to strip down more than once after a patient expelled some bodily fluid or another."

I frowned up and shuddered at the thought as I pushed the dark blue uniform shirt down her arms until it hit the floor. She undid her belt and pulled it free.

"Planning on using that?"

Without an answer, she looped it around my waist then tugged, forcing me to press up against her.

"I'd much rather feel your ass warming under my hand... If you're lucky," she added, throwing my wording back at me.

The image of me bent over, legs wide, and ass out while she landed gentle yet swift strikes seemed to be stuck on instant replay. Electric currents of excitement tingled under my skin as I thought of ways to make it happen. I leaned forward and caught the lobe of her ear between my teeth. I bit softly then flicked my tongue over the area.

"How bad do I have to be to get lucky?"

7

CHARLEY

THE BELT FELL TO THE FLOOR WITH A SOFT CLINK WHEN IT HIT the carpet. The swift smack to my ass stole my breath and opened the flood gates on my arousal. My heart beat so hard I was sure Ki could feel it from our close proximity. I pushed back into her hand that worked to massage the cheek she'd just spanked.

"Considering you're here and I still don't hear running water, I'd say you're gonna be pretty lucky." A lazy grin spread across her face and again, I didn't know if she was simply playing along, or really meant it, but I hoped it was the latter.

I scraped my teeth along my bottom lip and met her sparkling eyes.

Part of me wanted to hold out just to see what more she'd do. The hit to my ass had been unexpected, but fuck if it didn't set off a need I had no clue I'd had until that moment. But a bigger part of me wanted to have my hands on a very wet, very naked Ki.

"One shower coming right up."

I turned and sauntered off toward her bathroom, a tingle ran up my spine knowing she was probably watching the sway of my hips during my retreat. Water warming up, I secured my locs on the top of my head before rummaging under her cabinet in search of an extra shower cap.

"Great view."

I glanced back over my shoulder to see Ki, beautifully nude, and unabashedly staring at my upturned ass.

"The one I have is better," I said, standing with my plastic prize.

She said nothing as she grabbed her own cap from the hook on the wall and stepped into the steaming glass enclosure. I swallowed hard, before following suit.

Water glistened on her smooth, dark skin and I counted myself so lucky to be here in this moment with her. I leaned forward, Ki met me half way, taking my face into her hands and connected our lips. Soft and supple, yet strong and sure, they moved atop mine. Pressing closer, my pebbled nipples collided with hers and she thrust her tongue forward into my welcoming mouth. I moaned against the sensation, the gentle suckling of my tongue, the calm serenity of having her take the lead.

It was hard not to whine when she pulled back. Without a word she handed me her scentless body wash and sponge. Right. I was to wash away her stress. A job I happily tried to attend to. But she didn't make it easy. She drew patterns on my chest. Circles around my areola, across my cleavage, then over to the other side. The urge to lean against the tiled wall and get lost in the moment was strong, but that's not why I was here.

I focused hard on my task instead of Ki's hands. *Make her day better.* I massaged the sponge in my hands then started bathing her. The warm water pelted against my back and gave her skin a glossy sheen. I took my time cleaning Ki, enjoying the unrestricted access to her body. A wipe with the sponge followed by a second swipe with my bare hand.

I loved the heavy weight of her breasts in my palms and the

feel of her hard nipples when I ran my thumbs over them. I leaned in and kissed her. What was meant to be quick turned into a deep exploration of my mouth. The sponge dropped to the shower floor as I grabbed her hips. My body mashed against hers, one of her hands went to the nape of my neck, the other rested at my lower back.

The soft ping of the water pelting my shower cap mingled with our low moans as our kiss intensified. Pressure built between my legs, hot and throbbing. But what raged more was a need to watch Ki come undone and to know I'd been the reason. I wanted to please her. To make her happy. With that thought in mind, I broke from our kiss and air inflated my lungs. Our gazes remained locked, Ki slipped her tongue out and rolled it between her lips.

I massaged her hip before sliding one hand between our bodies, down over her slick abdomen until I reached my target. Coarse hairs tickled my fingers as I began languid strokes of my silken prize. A slow up then down, teasing either side of her clit, yet not giving full contact.

Ki's eyes fluttered closed, her mouth hung open, and she rested her head back against the tile wall. She kneaded and massaged my waist before she inched her hands down to cup my ass. She squeezed one cheek, then gave a swift slap which sounded louder, and stung more with the water acting as an amplifier.

I shuddered at the contact. My heart raced as I leaned in and licked the water running down the column of her neck. She widened her stance. I rubbed her stiff nub while licking my way down her chest. With my other hand I squeezed one breast, bringing it to my mouth. The tight bud was hard against my tongue as I flicked then suckled it.

Her breathing increased. I abandoned her breast and dropped to my knees. After hooking one leg over my shoulder, I spread her wide. I took a moment to marvel at the beauty in front of me before leaning forward and closing my lips around her. Using my thumb, I stroked her open folds and moved my tongue in circles around her hood. I moaned in delight, and greedily lapped at her sweetness.

Ki rocked her hips to match my speed. She held the top of my head as she gyrated against my tongue, moving and controlling my actions to hit where she needed it most. I wrapped my arm around the thigh on my shoulder, and I let her use me as she saw fit. Moving, circling, and dipping my tongue in and out of her body until tiny tremors overcame her.

Ki held me in place with one hand, the other scratched at the slick tiles. She bucked her hips forward then stilled when she took in a sharp breath before letting out a strangled whine. I slowed my pace, but kept contact, enjoying the swell of pride at watching the heaving of her chest and small spasms. I did that to her. My own pussy throbbed with pent up need for release, but I kept stroking her wanting to make sure she'd gotten all that she needed.

Ki looked at me with hooded eyes and a lazy smile. She lowered her leg, cupped my face to pull me to standing, then kissed me. Slow, controlled, but passionate. I shivered and it had nothing to do with the cooling water and everything to do with how much need ran through me.

My fingers twitched with the desire of more. To give her more. And as I slid my hand between her legs again, I focused my attention on her swollen clit. Languid easy circles. Our lips stayed connected. The kiss a perfect mixed of soft yet strong. Just like she was. Ki pulled back and rested her forehead against mine. I didn't stop moving. With our eyes locked on each other, she moaned and shook when the second round hit. Happiness swelled in my chest from fulfilling my goal to bring her pleasure.

Any thoughts of going for three were yanked away when Ki pulled back, and swiveled us so our positions were changed.

She turned me to face the wall and pressed against me. The heat of her body fought off the chill of the now cold water. I braced against the slick tiles and closed my eyes. A small whimper escaped when she pinched my nipples, tugging and tweaking them, not quite painful, but walking a close line. I loved it.

Pushing back, I pressed my ass to her crotch, rotating my hips and begging for the release that clawed under the surface.

She caught the lobe of my ear between her teeth. "You need something?"

I pressed my lips together and nodded. Ki continued to play with my breasts, rolling the tight nipples between her thumb and forefingers. The water beat down around us. The steam had long departed, but the heat radiating between us kept the chill at bay. Her hips moved in sync with mine as I gyrated against her.

She flicked my earlobe with her tongue then trailed kisses down the side of my neck. "Show me," Ki whispered.

I glanced over my shoulder at her. Ki's deep brown eyes locked gazes with my own before she moved in for a kiss. She swept her tongue through my mouth then pulled away. I gave chase, not wanting the all too brief connection to end. She covered one of my hands with hers. I tore my lips away from her to watch as she moved our combined limbs across my exposed tit. She made a slow circle with my fingers around my sensitive nipple.

I rested my head against her shoulder as she kissed the side of my neck while she maintained control. Abandoning my breasts, she moved down my stomach, inch by inch until she got to my needy pussy. It ached with unspent desire. When my fingers made contact, I let out a low whimper.

Reaching back, I touched her thigh and the side of her ass and squeezed. I pressed against her harder while I explored my sex with her in control of my movements. A "V" was made with our fingers, she leisurely stroked up and down on either side of my pussy.

Already aroused from getting Ki off, the electric need beneath the surface was close to breaking free. Snaking my free hand between our bodies, I made contact with her stiff nub as she continued to slide our joined fingers along my sensitive flesh. I rolled my hips against the action. I'd masturbated plenty, but letting Ki control the motion had to be the most sensually erotic thing I'd ever experienced.

Closing my eyes, I didn't think, I simply felt. The pinch and pull on my hard nipple. The smooth up and down, caressing my inner folds. I released a breathy sigh. Keeping focus on my actions was no easy feat, but I desperately wanted to bring her to climax again. I found an awkward rhythm just as my body stiffened. A seize. Ki pressed her thumb against my clit, the pressure acting as a release valve as my body gave way to shudders of pleasure.

"Oh, god, yes!" I rocked my hips faster and squeezed my eyes shut. The glorious freefall of euphoric bliss.

Behind me, Ki rested her head on my shoulder, her arm wrapped around my waist, and I felt the tremors of her body against me.

8

KIKI

I bit into the crunchy strip of bacon and watched Charley as she spread almond butter on her toast before topping it with a sliced banana. She placed a few strips on her plate, then moved to sit on the empty stool next to me. I couldn't stop the smile that tugged at my lips when she did a little shoulder dance with her first bite.

She turned to me, eyes bright, and dimple on full display. "So after you sleep, what do you want to do later?" She did another little shimmy. "Something that requires little to no clothing hopefully?"

Clothes, something she could barely be considered wearing. The oversized black and white striped tank that she either pilfered from her brother or an ex-boyfriend left large gaps on the side and hung low at the neckline. From any angle her breasts were on display giving damn near a full view of the small mounds. The only thing it effectively covered was her underwear-less ass.

I pressed my thighs together and did my best to ignore the many ideas that ran through my head at her suggestion. This thing, whatever it was with us, while fun, remained a little on the complicated side. Whether she wanted to acknowledge that fact or not. I took a sip of my coffee and tried not to choke on the black liquid. "We have to tell him."

The delightfully mischievous expression dropped from her face. Her lips tugged downward before she took a hard bite of her toast. As much as I tried, I couldn't stop the laugh. She was pretty damned adorable when she pouted. In response, she shot an angry side-eye glance in my direction.

"You know I'm right. I'm not down with hiding shit, are you?"

She huffed and leaned against the curved back of the stool. Her perky breasts were pushed up and sat atop her crossed arms. "I mean no, but is it really hiding, though? I haven't made a habit of telling Kenny about my hook-ups."

I took in a slow breath. *Hook-up.* Sure I'd had my share of one-nighters, and fuck buddies, so I couldn't begrudge her for having a similar mindset at this stage in her life. But as I was pushing thirty, that was something that appealed to me less and less each year. And it sure as hell wasn't something I'd planned, or wanted with Charley, not only because I felt a genuine connection with her during the platonic years, but also Kenny. Her brother and my long-time friend. The giant, invisible elephant in the room.

I was at a good place in my career, the promotion I'd gotten the month prior to shift supervisor meant I was on track to be department lead in a few years if I kept on pace. My schedule wasn't the most relationship friendly, but that didn't lessen my desire for something committed and serious. Did I ever imagine I'd be entertaining that path with my best friend's sister? Hell no. And yet I was, or wanted to. But Charley wasn't in the same place. And given the exchanges between us, we needed to be on the same page for quite a few reasons.

Hearing her use that word shined a spotlight on how ill-advised my course of action had been. I'd broken my self-imposed rule to not take things past platonic with Charley. The respect I had for my relationship with Kenny and the value I placed on both friendships had kept me from even considering any other possibilities. Not to mention being able to avoid what faced me currently. *Hook-up.* I picked up my coffee mug and took another gulp of the bitter liquid.

My mouth was as dry as the desert outside. I pressed my lips together and willed my voice to not betray the erratic beating of my heart. I hadn't been this pissed at myself in a long ass time. The little seductress managed to get under my skin and made me lose my fucking mind. "Even if this is...temporary, I'm not sure I could look him in the face and pretend nothing went on between us."

She sat up straight and pushed the back of my chair, making it swivel toward her as she turned to face me. "What the hell do you mean temporary?"

I startled at her apparent displeasure. "Uh, you just used the word 'hook-up.'" I made air quotes as I said the word. My own annoyance rising, fueled from my lack of sleep. "By design those are typically quick, non-committed, and short term. Hence temporary."

I turned my chair to the other side, grabbed my plate and cup, rounded the peninsula and walked into the kitchen. After dumping the rest of my coffee, I stared at the remaining strips of bacon on my plate. Even being annoyed, I couldn't in good conscience throw out perfectly good meat.

Charley snaked her arms around my waist and squeezed while placing a kiss on my back. "I didn't mean it like that. Just that I learned early not to discuss anything resembling dating around Kenny. You know how over the top he can be."

I turned to face her and rested my hands on her hips. Her light brown eyes held sincerity and I knew the truth behind her words. I'd made many a comment over the years that if he was that protective of his sister I'd hate to see how he'd act if he had a daughter. Over the top or not, I knew it came from a place of love and only wanting the best for her. As I did.

We'd only fooled around a couple of times. I could keep my hands and mouth to myself for the duration of her stay. It'd be less messy for all parties to end things before they got any more involved. Especially with her seemingly tapping into the dominate part of me that'd been dormant for far too long. Charley was young and still figuring herself out, she needed to do that. I thought the words, but my heart ached and my stomach knotted at the idea.

I wanted to be with her, and all her bratty eagerness. And while she claimed to want the same thing, I continued to have reservations about leading her down a path she might see as just a game.

Our bodies close, chests mashed together, her pebbled nipples collided with my own. *No getting distracted. I could do this.* "Your brother trusts me to take care of you."

A smile tugged at her full, soft lips. "You have, and I'm looking forward to you taking care of me some more." She winked and let her hands slide down until they grabbed my ass.

I cocked my head to the side and squinted. "That's not what I meant."

She nipped at my chin. "I know, but I like that thought better." Charley gave my ass another squeeze.

I raised a brow and she shrugged in response. "Still working out how naughty I have to be."

"You really are angling to be put over my knee." I was joking —mostly—but with the way her face lit up I recognized truth in her intentions. Maybe it was more than a curiosity with her. I filed the information away for later. That was a talk for another time.

Reaching behind me, I took ahold of her wrists and moved her arms so they were held between our bodies. "We need to decide what this thing between us is heading toward. And if it's going to be anything more than what we've already done, it needs to be upfront and out in the open."

Charley eased her hands free, crossed her arms, and took a step back. "So, this is like an ultimatum or something?"

I shook my head. "Nothing of the sort. I care about you and your brother. I care about the friendships I have with both of you and I care about the relationship the two of you have. Am I into you? Hell yes. And because of that I'm not willing to keep things on the DL and hide. Relationships take both people being on the same page with what they want and need."

I stepped closer and placed my hands on her cheeks and gave her a quick peck on the lips. "I'm going to get some sleep."

✳✳✳

Upstairs in the darkness of my room, sleep wouldn't come. My body was tired, but my mind raced and I couldn't shut it off. Was I giving Charley an ultimatum? Hiding, lying, and sneaking around took so much extra energy. There was no way I could look Kenny in the eye, or even talk to him knowing I was keeping something such big a secret.

I pulled the covers up over my head and groaned. It wasn't like I was making it out like she had to be the one to talk to Kenny. Hell, I could and would, once she gave the greenlight. Or we could do it together. The point was, if this was to be more, it needed to be open.

Still, the doubt gnawed at me. It curled around my insides and made my stomach ache. *Was I forcing my will on her?* I yanked the covers down when I heard the click of my door. Charley's shadowy figure padded across the room and stopped when she got to the side of my bed.

"Can I nap with you?"

Wordlessly, I lifted the bedding to invite her in. She climbed over and curled up next to me, resting her head on my chest, and let out a soft sigh. She slipped her hand under my shirt and spread her fingers out on my stomach.

"You said nap." I whispered the implied warning.

She wiggled closer, throwing her leg across mine. "I'm just getting comfy. I like the skin-to-skin contact."

I closed my eyes and let my fingers lightly trail up and down her arm. I willed myself to ignore the tickle on my thigh with each tiny move she made. Focus. Count sheep. Think about the schedule that I needed to complete for the next rotation. Anything to not dwell on the fact she laid beside me, leg over mine, and no panties.

Charley drew small circles with her finger tips. The barely there touch acting as a calming pattern, coupled with having her near me let the heavy blanket of sleep take over. She rocked her pelvis forward, bringing her heated center back to my attention.

Her voice cut through my pre-sleep haze. "I called Kenny."

My heart rate spiked hearing those three little words. I inhaled and let out the breath slowly. "And?"

"Not sure which he's more shocked over, that I'm dating you, or that I'm into women."

Shit! I hadn't even thought about that aspect. Not that I thought Kenny would have any issue, but my wanting to be in the open essentially meant she had to out herself. Fuck!

"Are you okay with that? I didn't even think…"

Charley shifted so that she laid on top of me. On instinct I wrapped my arms around her keeping my hands at the small of her back. She folded her arms across my chest and rested her chin on them. Even in the darkness I could see the bright smile on her face.

"It's all good. Besides I'm a growed up. He needs to see me as such."

I tilted my head to the side. "A 'growed' up. Um, yeah, using language like that is a sure fire way to show off your adult status," I said through laughs.

She did a one shoulder shrug. "Anyway, sure his mind is blown over the fact that I'm not a virgin, cuz double standards and all. But, now it's out of the way."

I rolled us so we laid on our sides facing each other and let out a sleepy sigh. "It is. But you know when I said we needed to tell him, I did mean 'we' as in you didn't need to call on your own."

Charley kissed the tip of my chin before snuggling down to get comfortable again. "I know. You always take care of me where Kenny is concerned. This time I could make you happy and showcase my growed up status to you. Aren't you proud?"

"Very proud." I hugged her tighter and let my eyes close. "Holy shit!" My sleepy eyes flew open when Charley shoved her cold feet between my legs. "How can those be like ice blocks when we live in the desert?"

She shrugged and pushed them under more. "I've always got cold feet."

I shifted so that I covered her frozen appendages completely. "Maybe try wearing socks."

She wrapped her arm around my waist. "Body heat works better."

9

KIKI

"YOU WANT TO WATCH ANYTHING IN PARTICULAR?" CHARLEY asked as she scrolled through the series options.

We'd gotten up after our nap, had a late lunch, and now sat relaxing on the couch, preparing to binge watch some TV. I stretched, readjusting my legs so they still covered her ice blocks. I'd seriously never come in contact with a person with feet as cold as hers.

"Whatever..." My reply was cut off by the ringing of my phone. Kenny's name flashed on the screen. I'd expected this call after Charley said she'd talked to him. I was dating his sister, if we could call it dating, more like exploring where things could go. With a long exhale, I slid the little green phone button over to answer.

"Hey." My gaze locked with Charley's.

She sat up, tucked her feet under her butt and mouthed "Is it Kenny?"

I nodded.

"Who started it?" The underlying disapproval mixed with a dash of accusation laced his tone.

"Why does it matter?"

Answering his question could have been the simpler approach, but his attitude booted me to the defensive.

"Because it does. That's my sister... I just never expected you to do something like this."

The hairs on the back of my neck rose to attention. I took a steadying breath, knowing in my heart of hearts a man I'd known half my life wasn't heading down that path. "Do something like what exactly?" I put my own underlying warning in my tone.

Silence. A long pregnant "is he in the car driving the two hours here to cuss me out in person" kind of silence. I pulled the phone away from my ear to verify we were still connected. Charley frowned and motioned for me to give her the phone. I shook my head and got off the couch. She followed me into the kitchen, parking herself on a stool and watched me.

Kenny let out an audible breath. "Nothing. I don't know. I guess out of all the friends I imagined trying to move in on my baby sister, you never crossed my mind."

"First off, I didn't 'move in' on your sister. Secondly, I'm woman enough to not try and hide shit from you. I respect you and our friendship way too much for that. When I realized there might be something between us, being up front with you was first and foremost."

"Yeah, yeah, and I appreciate that. But...that's my sister." Another long pause. "I'd hate to have to kick your ass for breaking her heart or some shit."

With that one comment all the coiled tension unwound. My chest could fully inflate with the breath of relief I took. I smiled in Charley's direction and gave her a little nod. The worried look on her face eased away.

"You could try, but I think I could take you."

Kenny barked out a laugh.

"I'm not out to break her heart. And listen, at least you never have to worry about me getting her pregnant and dipping out."

That comment made Charley tilt her head and purse her lips in confusion. After a few more verbal jabs back and forth I ended the call.

Charley tented her hands and tapped her fingers together. "So, I take it we officially have his blessing or whatever?"

I put my phone on the counter and nodded. She squealed and took the unconventional route of climbing over the counter to get to me, knocking the pendant lights in the process. Talking to Kenny, hearing he was okay with this did ease my worry. Most of it anyway.

I looked into her deep brown eyes. "Are you sure this is something you want to move forward with?" I don't know what made me ask. Maybe it was Kenny's shock or the feeling that I was still somehow betraying my friend, but the look on Charley's face told me she was not pleased.

She folded her arms and shifted her weight to cock out a hip. "I am, but apparently you seem to be the one with reservations."

I stepped forward and circled my arms around her slim waist. "It's not that."

There was another conversation to be had. One that would wait as Charley wrapped her arms around my neck and pressed her lips to mine. She slipped her tongue into my mouth, and I let my hands move down to her small, but firm ass. Kissing her was a delightfully addicting experience. Soft lips, moving tongues caressing each other, and low moans from both of us as the kiss deepened. My heart rate spiked. She wrapped her leg around mine and tangled her fingers in my curls.

Yeah, I was sure this was what I wanted. Had wanted, but did my damnedest to deny and ignore. Though rules needed to be put in place. Ones I'm sure she'd find creative ways to break. I pulled back. Charley licked her bottom lip before she broke out into a dimple revealing grin.

"We've told him, and he is okay with us. You can get on with the serving and protecting."

I rolled my eyes, and gave her ass a soft, playful smack. "I'm an EMT, not a cop."

The smile on her face widened. "So...playing doctor then?"

I laughed and shook my head. She wiggled out of my arms and quickly disposed of the oversized shirt she wore. My entire focus zoned in on her fingers as she drew circles around her light brown erect nipples.

"I mean, I could really, *really* use some hands on examining."

By gods she was beautiful. And now...no longer off limits. I was more than eager to do all the hands on examining she wanted. I tilted my head and appraised the sexy minx in front of me and an idea sprung forward.

"Besides the vibrator, what other goodies do you have?"

She stopped touching herself and her eyes grew to the size of saucers. Their warm, hazelnut color sparkled with amusement and shock.

"How do you know about that?"

I ran my tongue over the front of my teeth. "Well, I may, or may not have heard you that night."

Her shock gave way to flirtation. "And you didn't come join me?" She stuck her lip out in a faux pout.

I shrugged. "An error in judgement. One I plan on rectifying now."

Charley let out a squeal and bounced from leg to leg, her locs swinging free behind her. She grabbed my hand and yanked me towards the stairs. Once in her room, she all but skipped over to her bed. In the middle sat Rufus. I laughed quietly at the fact she not only still had the thing, but had brought it with her.

My attention went back to her when she bent over and pulled out a small, gray storage container from beneath the bed. "You brought your entire stash?" I asked, as I walked over and took a seat.

She plopped down beside me. "Better safe than sorry. I knew being under the same roof with you would make me extra horny. Plus, I didn't need Mom finding this when she undoubtedly went to deep clean my room now that I'm gone." She glanced at me, a coy smirk tugged at the corner of her mouth. "So, what did you do?"

"What? Do when?"

"When you heard me? What did you do?" She licked her lips, and lowered her voice. "Did you imagine me, legs spread wide, as I touched myself? Did hearing me get you all worked up and horny? Did you touch yourself?"

My body temperature shot up and the longing need between my legs intensified. Seductress indeed. "If you reenact the night for me, you can see for yourself."

With that she returned her attention to the plastic container. Three snaps and the lid came off. I peered over for a better look. It was quite the stash. Reaching in, I pulled out a silver chain with what looked like metal clothespins coated in black rubber connected to each end.

I raised a brow. "Nipple clamps."

She pushed her breasts together and pinched her nipples. "Haven't you noticed I like a little pain with my pleasure?" A quick air kiss in my direction before she released her breasts and reached into the box to pull out a bright pink vibrator.

I palmed the metal chain as she set the box onto her night-stand. The toy in her hand was slender, with a mid-sized bulbous tip. A smaller arm curved in the front and looked like butterfly wings. Reaching over, Charley pulled a wipe from a package and rubbed down the vibrator.

"This thing is the best! Hits my G-spot and stimulates my clit at the same time. I like the real thing, but this...this makes for a great substitute." She set it on the nightstand and stood in front of me. "You gonna use those?" she asked, jutting her chin toward the clamps in my hand.

10

CHARLEY

KI LOOKED DOWN AT HER HAND, SHAKING IT JUST ENOUGH TO make the chain rattle. I could barely contain my excitement hoping she'd say yes. Her eyes met mine briefly before she zeroed in on my hardened nipples. I shivered when she ran her free hand up my stomach until her thumb grazed across the tight bud.

"You want me to?"

I gave a decisive nod and she rose from the bed. Our gazes locked and I saw the hesitation there.

"You won't hurt me. I use them on myself all the time."

This was true. As much as I enjoyed a little pain with pleasure, I'd never quite trusted anyone else to take part in dishing out the pain aspect, aside from some playful spanking. Too many worries about completely letting go with someone you were casually hooking up with kept me from baring it all. There had always been something missing. Trust.

But with Ki, I wanted to experience that. I *could* experience it. A total surrender because as I stood face to face with her the missing link hooked between us. A bolt of thrill shot through me at the idea of it. The underlying urges that had been clawing for freedom beneath the surface were finally getting a peek at possible liberation.

"It's not about hurting you. Well, no more than you want to be hurt that is." She let her thumb graze across my nipple again and I arched my back into her touch. "What's your word?"

"I...I don't have one. I've never let anyone else..."

She kept running her thumbs across my nipples, teasing them, yet waiting. I searched my brain, then my eyes landed on my bed and a large grin spread across my face. "Rufus."

She laughed quietly and shook her head. "Rufus it is." Ki held my gaze for a moment longer before ducking her head to flick her tongue across a hardened peak.

I hissed when she lightly closed her teeth around it. The sensation was over before it started, but quickly replaced with another one when she placed the clamp on. After a repeat of attention on the other side, the absolute joy running through me was nothing short of exquisite.

I shivered when she ran her fingers down the valley of my breasts. I squeezed my hand into a fist when she took hold of the chain in the middle. My breath hitched and my pussy clenched in anticipation of the tug I so desperately hoped was about to come.

"Fuck," I groaned when she pulled it. Quick, but hard enough to increase the bite.

"Too much?"

I shook my head. "Not enough."

The slow grin that spread across her lips and the dilation of her pupils cranked up the need racing through me. She might actually be stepping into the role I needed her to fill. Ki snaked her hand behind my neck and pulled me closer.

Our mouths met in hard, rushed passion and I let go so she controlled the tempo. A muffled whimper passed my lips when she tugged the chain again. Bliss.

She held me in place but broke from the kiss. My head

swam, my nipples throbbed, this was heaven. I waited with bated breath for what she'd do next. Ki stroked the chain, letting her fingers glide back and forth, a small pull from one side to the next with each pass. The sensation enough to nearly make me come.

So close I could see the bobble in her throat when she swallowed, and feel the warm bursts of air when she exhaled. When she stuck her tongue out to moisten her lips, I wanted to get lost in the euphoria of kissing her again. But I waited. Waited for her to take the lead. To direct. To control.

Her fingers uncurled from the back of my neck, and I found myself missing the secure hold. She stepped back and lifted her arms. I eagerly complied with her silent request. In slow motion, I let my hands glide across her soft, heated skin as I raised the hem of her shirt. It was like unwrapping a present, and the anticipation of seeing what was hidden was almost as exciting as the reveal. Almost.

Torso bared to me, I leaned forward to kiss the side of her neck while my greedy hands palmed the weight of her exposed breasts.

"On the bed." The words were spoken in a raspy whisper.

The undercurrent of excitement rolled through me. Part of me wanted to disobey, to hope that my actions, or lack thereof would garner me that spanking—the real one—she repeatedly teased me with. But the bigger part of me wanted to do as I was told to make her happy. As I crawled onto the bed, knocking Rufus to the floor in the process, that part of me won out.

The low throb emitting from my nipples faded to the background and became a comforting ache. With slow, graceful movements, Ki climbed onto the bed, positioning her body just to the side of mine. She kissed me, leisurely and unrushed. I ran my hands up and down her smooth back. She rocked her crotch against my hip, I gyrated against her thigh nestled between my legs.

A low moan rumbled in the back of my throat at the increased pressure on my nipple when she pinched the clamp. Perfection. I arched my back, wanting, needing more. The second pinch brought my orgasm closer. I grabbed her leg, pressing it closer to my aroused sex, and circled my hips desperate for the contact to push me over the edge.

Ki broke from the kiss and lightly squeezed one of my tits. She ran her nose along the side of my neck and gave another light tug of the silver chain. The mix of pain and pleasure at someone else's hand—at her hand—was the key I'd needed.

"Fuck!" I cried out as the release I'd been chasing broke free. My fingers dug into her leg to keep her in place.

Ki lightly kissed my neck as she continued to rock against me. I let out a strangled cry when the pressure on my nipples lessened, then moaned as Ki licked and pampered them, replacing the minor pain with wonderful pleasure. It was an odd place to be aware of everything yet nothing all at the same time. Like being in a blissful state when you're not fully asleep, but also not really awake yet. A total out of body experience that calmed everything.

She continued to stroke and caress me while placing soft kisses across my chest before working her way up to my lips. She rolled us so I straddled her. I laced my fingers with hers and did a slow back and forth with my hips, rubbing myself against the only barrier between us. The soft cotton of her panties provided friction, but also blocked what I wanted most.

"Why are you still wearing these?"

My movements didn't stop. My overly stimulated nipples grazed against hers. I was acutely aware she'd put my pleasure before her own. *Again.* My heart swelled at the notion. I needed to return that favor. To thank her for what she bestowed upon me. If I could make her half as happy as she made me...I drew in a shuddered breath.

She tightened her fingers around mine and tilted her hips up. "Are you okay?"

A lazy smile spread across my face as I kept grinding against her, pressing harder for more contact. "More than okay."

I ran my tongue down the side of her neck before nipping at the tender flesh. Her lips parted and she let out a low sigh. Our hips moved in sync and I focused my efforts on giving back, showing my appreciation for all she'd done for me.

Ki widened her legs so I settled between them. Pelvis to pelvis, I kept rocking against her. My still aroused pussy tingled from the orgasm she'd given me. Wetness dampened her panties as I continued to hump her. Moving quick and deliberate with one thought in mind: bring her to climax.

Ki pulled her hands free, grabbed my head, and kissed me hard. An added thrill coursed through me from the tight hold of my hair and the domination of her mouth. She lifted, pushing her hips upwards and I circled faster atop her. She thrust her tongue into my mouth, and I welcomed the intrusion, moaning from the pressure and loving every moment.

She moved to grab my ass then pressed down, increasing the connection of our bodies. Tits smashed together, frantic movements of hips, my toes buried in the mattress for added leverage. I was close and her quickened breathing told me she was as well. Her fingers dug into my ass, and she dropped her head onto the pillow before she stilled and let out a low groan. I fisted the comforter as my second drop hit.

I rested my head on Ki's shoulder and she wrapped her arms around me. We stayed like that, each breathing heavy and waiting for the high to die down. After a few minutes I collapsed to the side, but snuggled close to her. I took comfort in the soft up and down of her fingers along my arm.

Her smooth voice broke through the silence. "How far down the path have you journeyed?"

I bit the inside of my cheek as nerves took place the of the euphoric post orgasm bliss. Letting my kink out in the heat of the moment was somehow much easier than talking about it. But this was Ki. She who I trusted. And she who rolled with it like a natural.

I swallowed the lump in my throat. "I've only ever used things like the clamps when getting off alone. But I liked you using them on me. Everything else has been online research. I found this one place, APX, it's like a club and from what I read it's a safe place to learn the ropes, so to speak. I've thought about joining, because safety first and all that jazz." My heart hammered even though I tried to sound as blasé as possible. I wanted this, her, to learn, grow and explore under her.

"What do you enjoy?" Her features remained relaxed. No judgement, no shock. Just calm, collected, Ki.

I shrugged. "I like a little pain, but nothing too extreme. So far." I bit the corner of my lip, might as well let it all out. "And being told what to do."

This time she laughed. "Now that is surprising. I've known you for a long ass time. Being obedient isn't a word I'd use to describe you."

"I've always listened to you."

Ki's laughter stopped at my declaration. She ran her thumb across my mouth before leaning down and giving me a chaste kiss.

"So, what exactly are you wanting from me?"

I twisted one of her curls around my finger and let my gaze drop to her lips. "To be my Domme," I whispered before looking back up at her.

She searched my faced and I saw the small bobble in her neck when she swallowed. "I've never held the official title. Though in past relationships, I guess you could say I took on those roles."

She was willing. I wanted to get up and do a happy dance,

but instead I moved to straddle her again. "I've done lots of research over the last two years, and we can do more together. But you're really okay with this? With being my Domme?"

She interlaced my fingers with hers. "Your Domme, huh? You're going to follow rules?"

I nodded quickly. "Most of the time, sure."

She laughed, rich and deep. "I wouldn't expect anything less. But research, because the last thing I want to do is hurt you. Well, more than you want me to that is."

I leaned forward and kissed her hard. "All the research you want."

EPILOGUE

Kiki

I WALKED INTO MY HOUSE TO THE FAMILIAR SCENT OF BACON AND coffee, but to the unfamiliar sight of Charley wearing pajama pants though the midriff T-shirt fit her general clothing options. Her freshly done locs were piled atop her head in a makeshift bun of sorts, secured with her multi-colored scarf as she loaded the dishes into the dishwasher. I was honestly surprised to find her up this morning considering she had been out late last night celebrating with her co-workers for making it through to the next round of her internship. Something that hadn't been the slightest surprise to me. She was as brilliant as she was bratty.

She bobbed along to whatever song played through the earbuds she wore. She jumped when my hands circled her waist.

"Crap you scared me," she said, pulling the buds free. Charley turned and gave me a quick kiss.

"Good morning to you, too." I picked her phone up off the counter and turned the music off. "I've told you, you're going to bust an ear drum listening to it so high."

She rolled her eyes and stuck out her tongue, which won her a swift smack to the ass. The coy smile that tugged at her lips told me that was probably what she was after. I could only shake my head as I moved over to take a seat. For the last few months we'd been navigating our new roles, and I'd surprised myself how easily I slipped into mine.

I'd paid for us to join the APX and it had been beneficial, though we still took things slow despite the fact she wanted to try more things and push her limits. It made me worried, but at the same time I had to trust she knew what she could handle. Topping from the bottom. A term I learned during our research, but fit the sexy minx in front of me to a tee.

She slid a cup of coffee toward me. "How was work?" She glanced at the clock on the microwave. "You're a little later than usual." She placed two slices of bread into the toaster then put a few strips of bacon on a plate. "Do you want eggs?" Charley was already heading to the refrigerator when she asked the question.

"Nah, I'm good. And yeah, I had to make a stop." I took a sip of my coffee and watched her briefly. "Be right back. I left something in my car."

The toast popped up. "Okay."

Once in the garage, I crossed the concrete floor in my sock covered feet and headed to the passenger side. I retrieved the carrier and closed the door with my hip. Inside Charley had set my plate next to my coffee mug and was seated on the other stool already enjoying her meal.

She stopped mid chew and tilted her head. "What's that?"

The bag shook and the small bark had her out of her chair and kneeling to peer through the mesh.

"Congrats, Doll." The new term of endearment I used

mostly during our play times, but I peppered into our day-to-day interactions because I loved having something special just between us.

She sat back on her heels when I unzipped the front and pulled the tiny, white ball of fur out. Charley sucked in a breath then let out a long squeal when I placed the puppy in her arms.

"Oh my god! Oh my god! Oh my god! You got me a puppy. A real, live, puppy."

The wonder and excitement sparkled in her beautiful brown eyes and my heart swelled from being the cause of it. She scrambled to her feet and with the puppy secured in one arm, she threw the other around my neck and peppered me with happy kisses.

"Thank you! Thank you! Thank you!"

Pure joy. That's what radiated from her, and it was downright adorable.

I rested my hand on her hip and let it slide down the curve of her backside. "You are most welcome."

Breakfast forgotten, she wandered off toward the couch, holding the puppy in front of her face so he licked her. I grabbed my plate and mug then went to join her.

"Babe, I can't believe you got me a puppy. He's so cute. And tiny. And cute. What kind is he?"

"A Bichon Frise. And I know how much you've always wanted a dog, so what better way to celebrate you making it to the next level of your internship."

She sat the tiny creature on the couch and he immediately ran over to me and sniffed at my plate. I quickly shoved the strip of bacon into my mouth before raising the dish out of his reach. He barked his displeasure.

"I'm not sharing bud, sorry."

"Aww come here fella, she's just a big ole' meanie." She stuck her tongue out again and I arched a brow in response. Charley cradled the pup in her arms. "Sorry, Miss."

I winked. "I'll let that one slide."

She continued to stroke his fur while I finished my food. "What should we name him?"

I shrugged. "Whatever you want. He's yours."

She held him up again, turning him from side to side before a dimple revealing smile graced her face. "Cyren!"

"Siren? Really?"

"Yeah, because you got him for me, and you know your job and all so cute right? But spelled c-y-r-e-n."

I tossed the name around in my head as I turned to put my plate down on the side table and pick up my mug. "I like it, Doll. Cyren it is."

She crawled over to me and gave me a quick peck on the lips. I shifted to make room for her as she settled against me, resting her back on my stomach. I ran my knuckles along her cheek and she turned into my touch.

I glanced down at Cyren who was dozing off in her arms. "I'm happy he makes you happy."

Charley cranked her head back to look at me and blew me an air kiss. "You make me happy."

She turned her attention back to petting Cyren and we settled into a quiet comfort. Which I knew would only last for so long because Charley liked to talk, about anything, everything, and nothing.

"Kenny called. He and Mom might come visit next weekend. They want to take me out to dinner."

"Sounds like fun."

She shot up and turned to look at me. "Oh shit. Cyren."

I set the cup back down and reached over to rub him behind his ears. "No worries. Hypoallergenic. Even though he'll live here, still thought it a good idea for reasons such as next weekend."

She gave me another megawatt grin. "If he's living here, I'm living here."

I leaned forward and kissed her shoulder. "All part of my masterplan." We hadn't officially talked about her staying here permanently, but none of our conversations ever brought up her moving whether she got the job or not.

She moved in for a kiss. "If that's the case, it's the perfect time for my surprise to you."

Before I could ask what, Charley handed me Cyren and moved to stand in front of me. She hooked her thumbs into the waist band of her pants and swung her hips from side to side. As she eased the thin, blue pants down, hints of deep purple peeked through. Once they were mid-thigh, my attention zoned in on the apex of her legs.

Against the rich plum color stood out white lettering with words: "Under" and a picture of a padlock underneath it. I tilted my head. Charley kicked her pants free then turned her ass to face me. The backside had: "And Ki" written above a picture of a key. It took me a minute to put it together.

She wiggled her ass. "You like?"

"I do." I sat Cyren on the couch and grabbed her wrist to pull her into my lap. "Under lock and Ki? Clever."

She circled her arms around my neck. "It's true, I am all yours."

"That you are."

THANK YOU

Thank you for purchasing Being Hospitable. I hope you enjoyed the story.

If you are so inclined, I'd appreciate a review at Goodreads and/or your place of purchase.

If you enjoyed this story, be sure to catch up with the other residents of Desert Rose Station in *Being Neighborly* and *Being Cordial*!

Until next time,

Meka

ABOUT THE AUTHOR

Meka James is a writer of adult contemporary and erotic romance. A born and raised Georgia Peach, she still resides in the southern state with her hubby of 16 years and counting. Mom to four kids of the two legged variety, she also has four fur-babies of the canine variety. Leo the turtle and Spade the snake rounds out her wacky household. When not writing or reading, Meka can be found playing The Sims 3, sometimes Sims 4, and making up fun stories to go with the pixelated people whose world she controls.

You can sign up for my newsletter at:
www.authormekajames.com

OTHER BOOKS BY MEKA

Being Cordial

*Book 3 of the Desert Rose Hookups

Being Neighborly

*Book 1 of the Desert Rose Hook-ups

Fiendish: A Twisted Fairytale

(*Please note this book tackles dark themes that may be upsetting to readers. You don't have to read Fiendish to read and enjoy Not Broken.*)

Not Broken: The Happily Ever After

*Continuation of Calida's story from Fiendish

The Lists

*Extended HEA for Calida and Malcolm from Not Broken

Anything Once

*Erotic romance featuring Ian and Quinn Faraday who are on a journey to spice up their sex lives

Made in the USA
Columbia, SC
24 June 2021

40981306R00050